LOS ANGELES CLIPPERS
ALL-TIME GREATS

BY BRENDAN FLYNN

Book design by Jake Slavik
Cover design by Jake Slavik

Photographs ©: Brian Rothmuller/Icon Sportswire/AP Images, cover (top), 1 (top), 21; Reed Saxon/AP Images, cover (bottom), 1 (bottom); Focus on Sport/Getty Images, 4; Focus on Sport/Getty Images Sport/Getty Images, 7; Kevork Djansezian/AP Images, 8; Chris Carlson/AP Images, 11; Mark J. Terrill/AP Images, 12; Alex Gallardo/AP Images, 15; Pat Sullivan/AP Images, 16; Jevone Moore/Icon Sportswire/AP Images, 18; Red Line Editorial, 22

Press Box Books, an imprint of Press Room Editions.

ISBN
978-1-63494-155-6 (library bound)
978-1-63494-168-6 (paperback)
978-1-63494-181-5 (epub)
978-1-63494-194-5 (hosted ebook)

Library of Congress Control Number: 2019951050

Distributed by North Star Editions, Inc.
2297 Waters Drive
Mendota Heights, MN 55120
www.northstareditions.com

Printed in the United States of America
012020

ABOUT THE AUTHOR

Brendan Flynn is a San Francisco resident and an author of numerous children's books. In addition to writing about sports, Flynn also enjoys competing in triathlons, Scrabble tournaments, and chili cook-offs.

TABLE OF CONTENTS

McADOO
11
BUFFALO
11

CHAPTER 1
BUFFALO ROOTS

The Los Angeles Clippers joined the NBA in 1970. But they weren't called the Clippers, and they didn't play in Los Angeles. They began as the Buffalo Braves. Upstate New York hadn't had a team since the Syracuse Nationals moved to Philadelphia in 1963. The NBA gave Buffalo a chance, and it worked for a while.

The Braves' first big star was center **Bob McAdoo**. In fact, he was one of the NBA's biggest stars at the time. McAdoo joined the Braves in 1972 and immediately won the NBA

Rookie of the Year Award. Two years later, he was the NBA's Most Valuable Player (MVP).

McAdoo won three straight scoring titles. He peaked at 34.5 points per game in his MVP season of 1974–75. He was an outstanding shooter and one of the first big men with a strong outside game.

Guard **Randy Smith** played more games in a Braves uniform than anyone else. He's also the franchise leader in points. He averaged 17.8 points per game and was a two-time All-Star with the team.

HOT-SHOT ROOKIES

The Braves had two other NBA Rookies of the Year besides McAdoo. Point guard **Ernie DiGregorio** won the award in 1973–74. Shooting guard **Adrian Dantley** won it in 1976–77.

Buffalo made the playoffs three straight seasons. But eventually the Braves were sold and the new owner moved them to the West Coast.

MANNING
5
MASON
14

CHAPTER 2
GO WEST

The team moved to San Diego, California, and was renamed the Clippers in 1978. After missing the playoffs six straight seasons, they were on the move again. This time they skipped up the Pacific coast to Los Angeles.

In Los Angeles, the Clippers had to fight for attention with the Lakers, who were in the middle of an NBA dynasty in the 1980s. The Clippers finally had a star of their own when they selected forward **Danny Manning** with the first pick in the 1988 NBA Draft. He had just led Kansas to the college basketball title and was one of the biggest names in the game.

Manning's time with the Clippers was plagued by injuries, but by his fifth year he was an All-Star. He averaged 22.8 points per game that season, doing most of his damage with a strong low-post game.

The Clippers later added two more college stars, both from Duke University. Swingman **Corey Maggette** averaged 17.3 points per game in eight seasons with the Clippers. Power forward **Elton Brand** spent seven years in Los Angeles, scoring 20.3 points and grabbing 10.3 rebounds per game. Together, they led the Clippers to the playoffs just once. They won a first-round series over Denver in 2006 before falling to Phoenix in the conference semifinals.

MAGGETTE 50

BRAND 42

STAT SPOTLIGHT

CAREER FREE THROWS

CLIPPERS TEAM RECORD

Corey Maggette: 3,122

GRIFFIN
32
STAPLES
SLAM DUNK
KIA

CHAPTER 3

LOB CITY

Clippers fans finally had a lot to cheer for when a number of talented young players arrived to form the core of an exciting team. The breakout star of that group was power forward **Blake Griffin**. The 2010–11 NBA Rookie of the Year was an All-Star in each of his first five seasons.

Griffin averaged a double-double in his first two NBA seasons. He scored more than 20 points per game in all but one of his eight seasons with the Clippers. Griffin was best known for his dunking abilities. He famously won the 2011 All-Star Slam Dunk Contest when he threw one down after jumping over a car.

The Clippers acquired point guard **Chris Paul** in 2011. That helped earn the Clippers a new nickname. Paul excelled at lob passes that set up his teammates for spectacular dunks. So fans began calling them "Lob City."

Paul was already a four-time All-Star when he arrived in Los Angeles. He made five more All-Star teams as a Clipper. A strong shooter, he averaged nearly 19 points per game over six seasons in Los Angeles. Paul also won four NBA assist titles, including two with the Clippers.

PLAYOFF PUSH

The Lob City Clippers made the playoffs six consecutive seasons. Though they only won three series over that span, it was still quite an accomplishment. The franchise had only made the playoffs seven times in 41 previous seasons.

PAUL
3

JORDAN
6

Center **DeAndre Jordan** was on the receiving end of many of Paul's dazzling passes. Jordan was a second-round pick in 2008. He quickly established himself as one of the league's top centers. In 2013–14 Jordan began a string of seven seasons averaging a double-double. He won the NBA rebounding crown twice and led the league in field-goal percentage five times. Jordan's rebounding skill landed him on the NBA All-Defensive first team in 2014–15 and 2015–16.

STAT SPOTLIGHT

SINGLE-SEASON REBOUNDS PER GAME

CLIPPERS TEAM RECORD

DeAndre Jordan: 15.2 (2017-18)

LEONARD
2
CLIPPERS
2

CHAPTER 4
MODERN STARS

After years of futility, the Clippers finally were competitive with the Lakers in the crowded Los Angeles market. The success of the Lob City crew helped attract a new generation of superstars to join the Clippers.

Kawhi Leonard won his second NBA title in 2019 with the Toronto Raptors. The 6'7" forward scored a career-high 26.6 points per game that season. Then he carried the Raptors to their first championship. Leonard was the prize of the free agent class that summer.

He had plenty of options for where to sign. He chose the Clippers.

Leonard's presence in Los Angeles drew the attention of other NBA stars. It likely played a big role in the Clippers also being able to acquire high-scoring forward **Paul George** before the 2019–20 season.

SUPER SUB

Guard **Lou Williams** had played 12 seasons in the NBA before he joined the Clippers in 2017. He certainly found a home in Los Angeles. He had never averaged 20 points per game in an NBA season. Then he did it twice in a row with the Clippers. He was named the NBA's Sixth Man of the Year both seasons.

A six-time All-Star with the Pacers and Thunder, George was coming off a career year. He averaged 28.0 points per game for Oklahoma City. He was named All-NBA and All-Defensive first team and finished third in league MVP voting. Fans hope his long-range shooting and

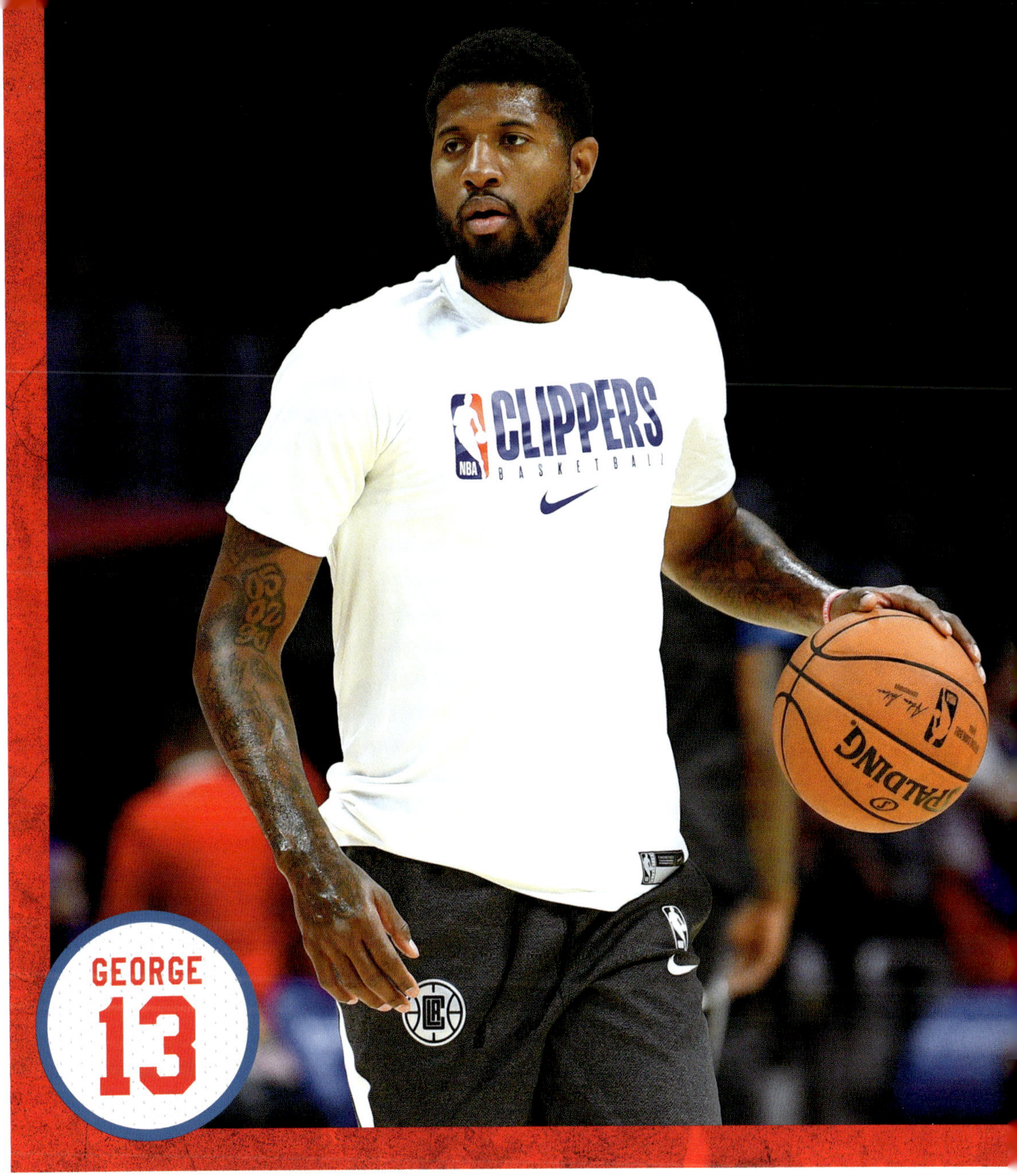

strong defense will complement Leonard's all-around game for years to come.

TIMELINE

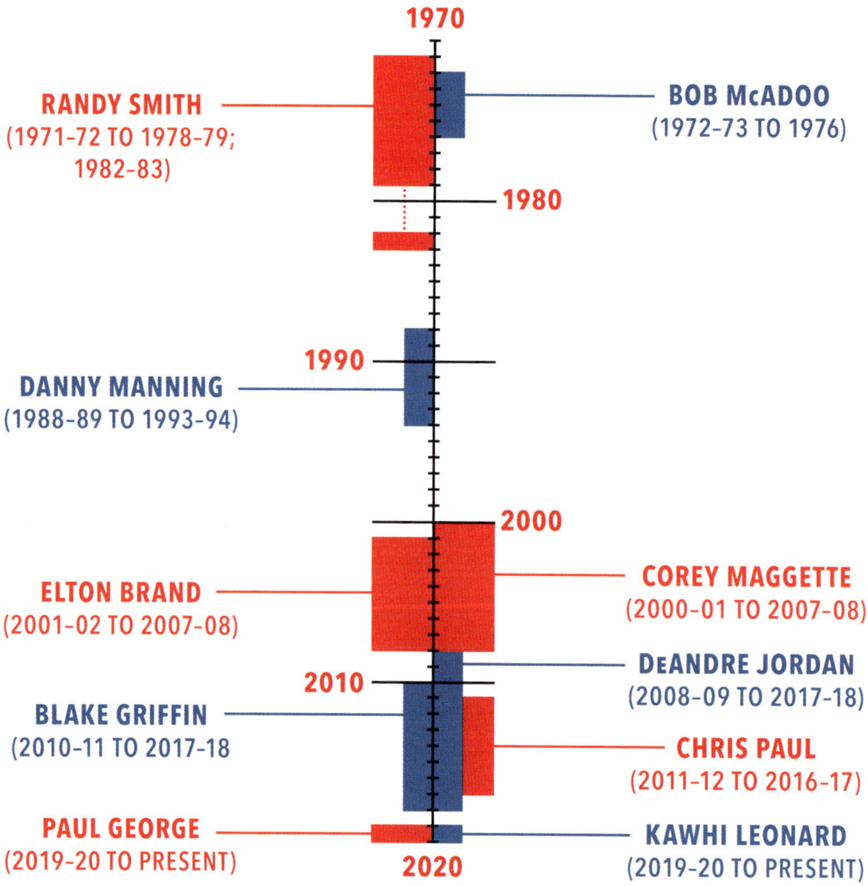
1970
RANDY SMITH
(1971-72 TO 1978-79;
1982-83)
BOB McADOO
(1972-73 TO 1976)
1980
1990
DANNY MANNING
(1988-89 TO 1993-94)
2000
ELTON BRAND
(2001-02 TO 2007-08)
COREY MAGGETTE
(2000-01 TO 2007-08)
DeANDRE JORDAN
(2008-09 TO 2017-18)
2010
BLAKE GRIFFIN
(2010-11 TO 2017-18
CHRIS PAUL
(2011-12 TO 2016-17)
PAUL GEORGE
(2019-20 TO PRESENT)
KAWHI LEONARD
(2019-20 TO PRESENT)
2020

TEAM FACTS

LOS ANGELES CLIPPERS

Formerly: Buffalo Braves (1970–71 to 1977–78);
San Diego Clippers (1978–79 to 1983–84)

First season: 1970–71

NBA championships: 0*

Key coaches:

Mike Dunleavy (2003–04 to 2009–10)
215–326, 7–5 playoffs

Jack Ramsay (1972–73 to 1975–76)
158–170, 9–13 playoffs

Doc Rivers (2013–14 to present)
307–185, 20–26 playoffs

MORE INFORMATION

To learn more about the Los Angeles Clippers, go to **pressboxbooks.com/AllAccess**.

These links are routinely monitored and updated to provide the most current information available.

**Through 2018–19 season*

GLOSSARY

complement
To work well with something else.

double-double
Accumulating 10 or more of two certain statistics in a game.

dynasty
A team that has an extended period of success, usually winning multiple championships in the process.

established
Showed to be legitimate.

franchise
A sports organization.

free agent
A player whose rights are not owned by any team.

lob
A pass to the rim that allows a teammate to catch and dunk in one motion.

plagued
Damaged.

rookie
A first-year player.

sixth man
A player who comes off the bench but often plays as many minutes as the starters.

swingman
A player who can play both guard and forward.

INDEX